Printed in the United States of America

First Printing, 2020

ISBN: 978-1-7347545-7-5

Press Here
410 S Michigan Ave Suite 420
Chicago, IL 60605

www.mattbodett.com

Cover artwork by
Megan Sterling
www.megansterling.com

THAT
WHICH

Dedication

The drop.

This book is dedicated to reasons.

Especially.

It began as a way to understand sorrow. I was not born to be a virtuoso. Nor could I be called one now. But, I can play a song the way the wind teases the crest of a wave.

When is truth delusional?

Orpheus was the name of my father. That's a weight I was destined to carry. I nudged it, a stone in my pocket, until its smooth edges pierced my side. It could have been something more than sorrow, more than the depths of hemlock, but it turns out that the way to comprehend the salt of tears is to taste the bitterness of sand.

When I tell others of my ancestry they deem me a liar. I want to be one. I want to sing beyond the ribs which encompass a sense of longing. Instead, my presence ensures the length of pain which equals a prescription of Zyprexa.

It is okay.

I say that sometimes to make you feel better about your choices. I say that sometimes to make myself feel better about not caring where my eyes rest on the horizon, or where my feet ache to plant.

Sometimes, when I rest in the day room, I recognize the scent of caring. Or possibly the dust of reckoning.

I could write a song now. I could press wine into the ear and produce a honey sweeter than manna. I could write a few lines at least. Will you wait. Do you have the patience to wait until the dust settles?

Be
Longing

Exists the moment before. Not yet the ripple.

1. It was soft like the way you hold in crying around other people. It was rain like the way other people cast shadows. It was a way of holding the house when there wasn't a reason to leave. Each moment a way of holding the next. I sat, trying something more than the news I had been broken this whole time. Realizing that (other than) now was impending upon (my) now. I slipped back into the ruffle of ideas beside desk beside bookcase beside bed inside room. I comforted back into something like a blanket that was nothing like a blanket, but more like a knowing. This was how I spent my day.

2. My shoes were slightly larger than one half a size and scraped the sidewalk/cement in a way that reminded me I was still one step behind myself. In a hurry to catch up I found the signal to walk and scurried past the non building that was construction, its holes big enough for a life. The continued river of moment filled my mind, and in that I belong to the inquisitive nature of filling.

3. Aching found a place amid highways and buildings and somewhere I cast a shadow that stretched into the darkness of another shadow. I could not recognize the source, but I liked the shape. Melding pasts we both became the next and not knowing. We became, then parted. I do not know what the name for that is.

4. Looking forward and slightly to the side, I planted a stick in the sand. I know that there is no future tree in the planting, but the action became an overture to

the day. The branch being exactly what it was. It was neither growing nor dying. Its purpose planted firmly in the softest portion of sand. Its exactitude being a monolith to the notion of belonging. I knew I wanted to be like this stick, planted and soft and firm in what or why and neither dying, and what is the notion they refer to when they say "just do it" or "expatriated"? Either way I delved into knowing that somewhere beyond the sandy length there was another stick that reached out beyond the tree it fell from and wanted, like me, to be firmly and belongingly.

5. I returned home and said to the vacancy that my return was not to be mistaken for anything else. We were in agreement, or its lack of response belonged with nothing and before exactly. I fell asleep knowing I could not be contained in its need for filling.

If exactly is then why is not

Belonging to the moment of precision. Deafening silence is the sound of hitting.

"Why would I?"

Because we saw the way of flying in the moment of throwing. Not the release, but in the eye, the length, the idea of destination.

"The destination? I do not know the name of that."

Neither do I.

"What do we know?"

What is stronger than simply. What is becomes the superlative that underscores all isms. Is that what you are looking for?

"I no longer know. I want to secure the idea before I plant each foot. I want to be sure. I want to know why."

Why is not what. Why does not plant. Why provides but does not end. And in end there is no. Another glance at that place and we see that we knew only why and not exactly and not moment of. When each heart beat belongs in other than it cannot nourish, it only passes on to. Each moment wants to be wanted. Each wanting seeking more than longing and precisely belonging. We are the exactly. Not in time, not in seeking, not in that/this, but in. And now you touch the very core of it. The expansion is not moving. It is recognizing. You do not find new things. You familiarize.

"Have I known before?"

Before? no. Now. Yes. Before/now. Yes.

Planting the moment of

Singing the highlights of creating. The drop is not drop, but in separation.

Marching forward across the day I realize that I sang into every moment a breath that belonged to someone else. My moments belonging to the other thing that was rich, but still not my own. I wanted to bring that rhythm into life, making a creation of the ration. I knew that my arms could only stretch to eight feet and the ceiling was ten. Beyond the clamoring of the white painted threshold I could feel energy, like a tree expanding from a seed, a thousand times, a thousand more. Each seed belonging to the cycle it proclaimed, and each cycle knowing it was not a cycle, but a way. Each way was knowing that the end was exactly the destination, so that each sight could see and each breath could separate.

I planted a stick in the sand. A stick like a seed. Not in shape but in purpose. In purpose the stick was everything I feared to say because in the speech I would recognize each character, and each character would mean something more than was. I stood and stared at the stick. Knowing that saying would negate the purpose, I lost the words intentionally and sought to become like the flakes of bark that hung on to not-a-purpose. I became brown and scaled. I became both the air end and the sand end. My length shared its ratio to the planted moment of reasons.

I sometimes cannot feel the things that others do. I think the stick relates. Being planted in something that finds itself as a purpose, as a place to be something that finds things planted. I swirl amid those thoughts and circle to the location of seeing something outside the planted stick. Several feet away there is grass. The grass is slightly green, slightly brown, petrified in between the air end and the sand end. The life end and the death end. The breathing end and the not breathing end. The breathing becoming the not breathing only in shape but not in purpose. Like a seed.

For the moment, I would like to explain that I do not understand the crescendo of experience. I do not comprehend the vast inside the feeling of space, like filling. Instead I walk along the notion of aspect and point to decayed theory and broken sounds that explode into momentary fertile slats. Slats like formations of staggering. Or moments of. Or moments. And in this moment I would like to explain that I do not understand the crescendo of experience.

Faltering is my forward.

I was walking along a beach. On a path by the beach. The path had been made some time ago. It was remarkable to look at. I was walking along it and I could see many other people enjoying the way the sun became a part of how we experience the day. It became the thing we sought out, despite its distance. Catching only a moment of its trace was enough for all of us on this one day. I was walking on this path and my hair could feel the passing brush of the breeze. The breeze that quenched a curiosity for flying, or floating, or falling. I felt that breeze and held each chapter of it deep inside my understanding, as if a bookmark could hold a thing called place. The breeze became my understanding of what that moment felt like, because it engaged me unlike the sun. It allowed me to understand it, unlike the path. I floated along and when I reached a point I turned into the sand and each step sank, only until the depth of exactly and then it fingered its weight around. The waves became the visible breeze. The tactile floating. They effortlessly moved between each notion of here and still found their way across the terrain of longing. They became the moment of here and here and here. Ebb became the word that moment felt like.

I touched the sand. Not every sand, but the sand that lived between the air end and the wave end. That sand was saturated with offering and purpose. I touched that sand and its coarseness reminded me that the breeze was soft and that the waves were neither soft nor harboring. The sand reminded me that the waves were.

I was walking along a beach. On the sand by a beach. I found a fish there. The fish had died, I don't know when, but it was being consumed by the seagulls. I watched the dance, like beauty seeking a reason. They shifted with the sounds, and the waves clapped in rhythm. The sharpened beaks perched on the flesh of the fish and struck against themselves in crowd. Longing for companionship they devoured existence like the crumbling of a path. Their eyes became mine and in unison exited stage left. The poor corpse, locked with mine, went nowhere. It became the wave end. The air end. The end end.

I softly kicked the sand around as I beckoned the breeze beyond the moment I became a part of. The onerous weight of the sun shifted my covering. And out of the front of my vision I found a stick. A stick that was floating, not on breeze like time, but through. A stick that looked so unlike a boat that it was nothing like a dance. It could not caress the carcass like the seagulls. This stick simply washed up. Washed up to my feet. I stared at its clumsy adoration and touched it like the sand. It reminded me that the waves were neither here nor there nor here or here or here or here. I watched as the saturated weight lifted from inside the stick and its dry skin exposed its flavor. I longed to know about the stick, where it had been, where it wanted to be, and why it wasn't. I held the stick, as if wanting to learn from it the skill of flying. It moved effortlessly through the air, even when I never let it go. Even when there was no name for destination.

I planted the stick in the sand. Like a seed. Not in shape but in purpose. In purpose the stick was everything I feared to say because in speech I would recognize each character, and each character would mean something that was more than. I stood and stared at the stick. I forgot to need a reason. As if there was something I could do or say to make it alright. I became both the air end and the sand end. My length shared its ratio to the flavor of the breeze. Flavor became the way that moment tasted.

its moment is

The rational portion of it. The drop is not.

The diagram belongs to something of a sense. In the sense belongs prolonged understanding. Spend time, and sense, and sense. Each moment a realization that you are in and beyond, simultaneous and finding. With closed eyes providing the curtain of suspended belief. Beyond. You can sense grasp.

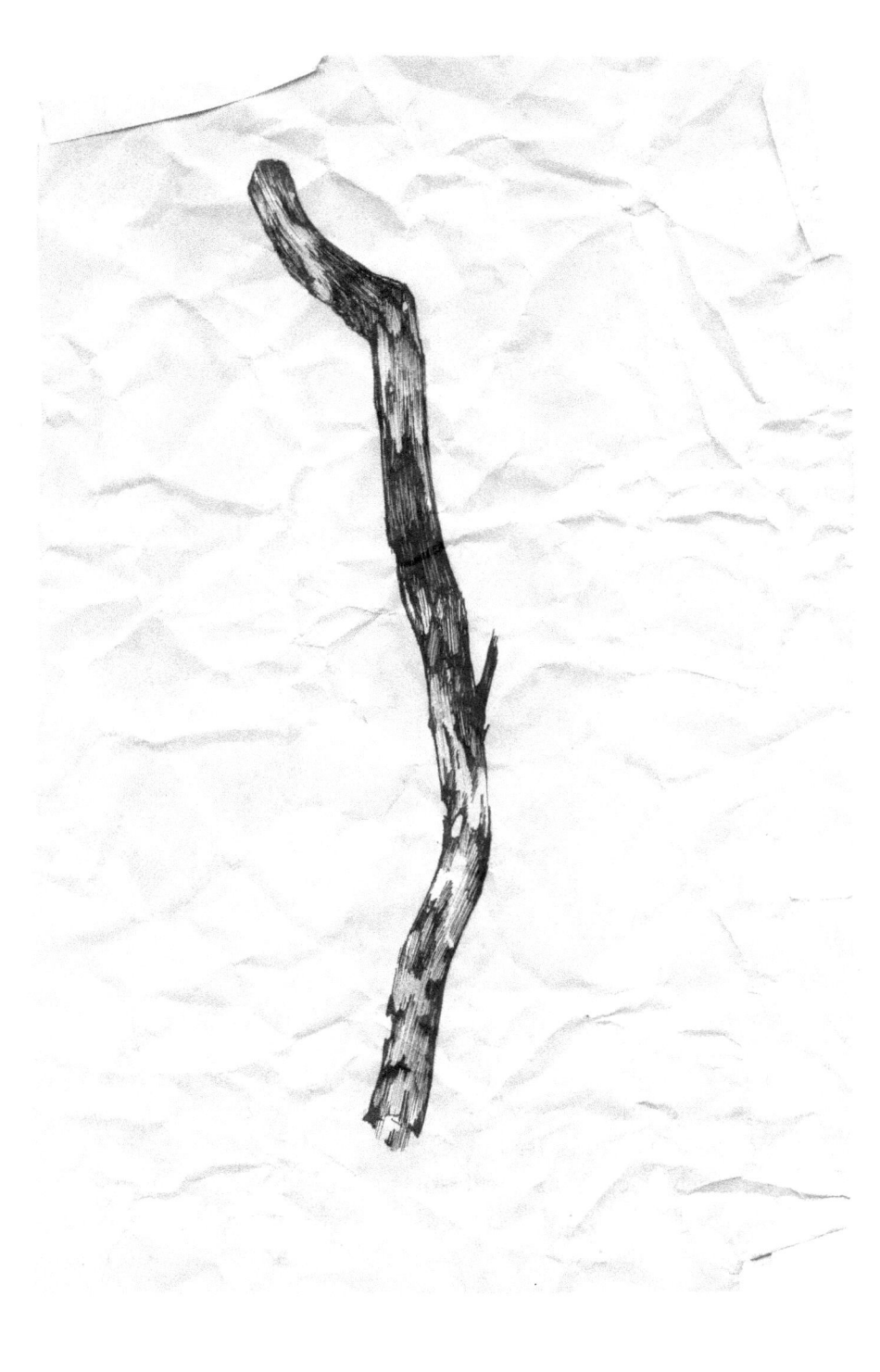

The Promethean sense. Belonging to the gods and championing the decay. Cheering the stuff of nothing because it will extend beyond beyond because it can embody. Containing all ends simultaneously. We give all to the humanity because its surging sails beyond purpose. It is more than not thing and touches less than everything (air end).

to belong to (yours is most this)

Any number of years now. Drop extends through limitations and proportions

I was walking on the beach. On a path to be more exact. And its length was limited to the materials on hand, but its idea wrapped itself beyond cave or length. I was walking on the beach and I found a stick.

"Where was it?"

It was at the end of my reach. Just finding the sensation of connection. It was there and I was more beside, and knowing that there could be nothing outside or moment. I belonged to precise. I saw it there. The soft ebb of my heart pushing tomorrow through my veins. The breath that filled my chest belonged to stick and wave. It was not mine, but its gift made mine exact then precise and knowing.

"Sometimes the sun hurts. My eyes and my skin."

And the stick saturated with wave becomes the metaphor for believing. The sun not hurting, but process. They act in accordance to each other. The supple warmth of gaze procures the life that is somewhere, inside, perhaps not lost, like teeth or innocence, found like strength and flavor. I watched as the saturated weight lifted from inside the stick and its dry skin exposed its flavor. That is what I told myself. That is what I wanted to feel.

"What does it feel like?"

Like name. Like safe or maybe not safe, but more the

way soft feels when dust settles. Knowing that neither this nor that can interfere. Apprehended ideas firmly give way to settled notions.

"Have I known before?"

Before? No. Now. Yes. Before/now. Yes.

The Pulse of Not Quite

Interlocking parts are still parts. The drop is still a drop.

Two simultaneous moments: Out and In

I walked along a path. The path was on the beach and it surprised me how the sun felt as it ripened my skin. Each precise being what was needed, and yet the looking was white with searching. I found my way, feet first to the sand and the waves and the stick. I do not understand the crescendo of experience. But I know that something about the breeze combing my hair felt similar to being wanted. I like how that felt. In fact, I knew how that felt because that is what it felt like to to balance precariously on knowing there is nothing to say. Each character becomes more than something. Each lullaby plays its familiarity in my mind. I know what was and what was needed.

Where are the longing/ and belonging/ and something about motion? I preemptively provided you with all the pertinent information because that is how I know. I know/ like you know/ like matter and strength/ and take a breath/ each time/ each time/ like that/ because you know that living is made of the precision of knowing/ and take a breath/ and take a/ knowing that precision is exact (by definition) and/ I am here to remind you that breath is like that stick/ its length is neither/ nor/ and ends with / and in/ and capacity knows what it is like to need something/ I have a longing/ In Be/ and precise/ and I want to understand the concept of filling/ because I know that

I knew it all again. My breathing was someone else's, it was yours. And when I realized that the breathing was yours I recognized that you were beside and in, and through the moment we both see and become an end. Air end and sand end. And the stick still, not being tree or dead, not being precision was us even though we were not more than.

Each word described something. I cannot subscribe to this. Each word is more than exact. Each belongs to this and notion and periphery. Each word is working toward the things of nothing and want. Like capacity that feels. I long to know.

Scratching the bewilderment from the crown of today. I woke and read. Each reading filled with characters. Each character meaning something more than.

yesterday you touched me and it felt like filling/ like the sun/ or like wave/ like a love that has to be explained/ in a moment they find a path to describe their direction/ and direction is a limited idea/ beyond is limited to direction/ and yet beyond is precisely not the exact/ take a breath here/ and there is a notion of tomorrow in the way the breeze/ breath/ takes on the brush/ there is a notion of tomorrow/ in the way I take on the/ stick to the path and find/ but limited/ and supple ideas find the sand/ simile/ or metaphor/ and breath/ and now we have something called progress/ can you see it now?/ I admire your tenacity/ and your description of love like a bad metaphor/ it always gets used again/ but what is it like to go beyond/ yond/ and er/ and end./ Suppose that we can feel the friction

Each creative endeavor of finding became a momentary ebb, though each moment became simply the next. This was how I spent the rest of my day.

I walked out the door that day. The sun was warm against my skin and felt like the way a blanket wraps. The blue waves of the sky undulated into a breeze and I felt, for a moment, that I was. And inside I knew that there could be. And outside I kept walking.

The grey of the sidewalk gave way to traffic and feet and garbage.

I noticed the particularity of garbage and it became something beautiful and lasting, not in purpose but in shape. Its cast-off became mine. My shadow could not be released from my side and yet its shape was

of/ lasting/ and is there a way to stop/ or is there a way to ask a question that does not include a mark?/ like that/ there was a mark/ but is there a way to ask a question and make it last longer than

like that.

similar. Its length shared its ratio to the planted moments of reasons. My reasons felt and grass protruded between the gaps and. The garbage became how the walk felt that morning. The garbage became how the reasons found.

I went for a walk that morning and found reasons in shapes and becoming in cast-off. And the sidewalk path became an asphalt and the asphalt had cracks and the cracks had grass, then sand fell away to present. And I walked off the edge to see if sand could hold the weight of the day, and it faltered, its forward, and was holding me toward the rhythm of wave and wave and wave. Ebb was how my heart felt that moment. If there was a word to describe this I would use it here, but nothing is too much like something. Belonging used to be something else and moment is narrow enough to let the sun remain warm. On my skin it rests and the characters of thing become nothing like their definitions.

Take a breath here/

Not to yield

Falling, not from force, but from will. Drop knowing destination.

I was walking along a beach. On the sand by a beach. I found a fish there. The fish had died, I don't know when, but it was being consumed by the seagulls. Its belly heaved toward the waves. Interlocking scales resisted, then gave way. I could sense loss. And purpose. The singing of gulls wracked the moment with torture or not torture, but more like a cycle that knew its own end. I could see lost in the fish eye and harmony in the birds. What does harmony feel like when it comes at a cost. A question without a mark. A knowing without a simplicity. All moments become this, seeing beyond, captured in a cavity. A hollowness inside a thingness. It was a fish, but no longer, and it became the cycle it wanted so badly to avoid.

When you see the feeling through the thing, no longer the important. I shared this with a friend who laid on the beach. On the sand by a beach. Died, I don't know when. His efforts became my sight in a single moment like a pause. I do not understand the crescendo of experience. And yet, the periphery opened to find me knowing what flight felt like in the presence of hollow weight.

The sun was hot, and warm, and there to make comfort palpable. Linked across all the knowing. The sun became a part of how we experienced the day.

I watched the dance, like beauty seeking a reason. The gulls shifted with the sounds, and the waves clapped in rhythm. The sharpened beaks perched on the flesh of the fish and struck against noise and wave and beak and clasped tightly. Their eyes became locked with mine. The poor corpse went nowhere. I devoured the flesh with the sharpened beak of familiarity. Not from harm or disgust. Not from yester or searching. I devoured the flesh with a blanket like kindness, finding sensation in holding.

Tomorrow I may understand this and how it hurts or doesn't hurt, or how the sun or not the sun, like my skin knows neither the heat nor the moisture.
There is something to belonging that a dying fish can comprehend. Stretched across cycles of years. The fish of us can sense a part of wanting the sun and getting the rain. Each drop swelling to the size of.

Making the choice

Singled as abrasive. Drop is something bigger than before.

It was before walking that the day began. It was before the ripening of yawn and stretch. The curious sounds still distant in the ear. The slats of blinds keeping sight from reaching the day beyond. One small crack in the barrier letting in a sliver of sun become the pierce in the side. The vinegar of dawn distilling all dreams.

I woke to the piercing of my side, proceeding toward my eye. Its awkward nature became the beginning. Fumbling around in nakedness I found a sheath of cloth and pulled importance into my day. I longed for a noise to shatter something but instead found that my nose could only sense not sound. Still I reached the door and the frame and the beyond and the next room became the same longing. I found myself now knowing, and wanting, and needing to fill.

There is a point in the day when, soaked with water, we cleanse the old. The knobs cranked to provide something warm and hot enough to deter building up. Washed away. The steam creasing itself around the curvature of form, planted into delicacy and ephemeral. At all moments steam knows exactly its purpose. To rise and saturate and ebb and dance to all things present and moving and breathing. And there I stood. Dumbfounded by the sense of all as before and new. Its rotation completed by the ending and prepared for again.

Turning off the water I sensed each curling bead holding on until avoidance was no longer the option.

Dropping around and through they found their way to place and fulfilled exactly. Each bristled end of the towel soaked the remainder and placed nothing. It supplanted notions of empty where there was nothing to hold it. And I continued without notice. I continued because day was day and everything happened. It was all precise and scheduled. Even the way my clumsy interacted with grace was not off key.

Each wet footprint left an indication of past, and each evaporated fragment indicated future. I slipped into non nakedness and covered sense with security. This was normal.

It was in my non naked state that I stood before myself, not in shape but in purpose. Characters formed into words and they formed into things called sentences, and they formed into things called thoughts, but I do not understand what they become after that. They are idea, but idea does not answer to form or character. It was in the latter that I discovered that not knowing was all I could present. It was in this fever that I stepped beyond the threshold. I stepped onto sidewalk and my shoes were slightly larger than on half size and scraped the cement in a way that reminded me I was still one step behind myself.

Lesson in flying

Prolonged understanding produced akin. Drop drop drop is more than drop.

"What is the meaning?"

A breath. A way of breathing. I can do headstands now you know. Its about the effort of trying and balance and falling. In the moments between the height and the floor. I understand flying. Or at least desire. That is meaning. The desire for. The desire.

"What do you do now?"

In between I know and figurative speech I reconcile problems. Mostly my own notions, but also placement, like bricks and stones. I seek understanding through weight and not texture. All beings lasting by lengths of time or consequences to ebb.

"Like the wave?"

Like the wave. Its consequence increasing to the next wave. Its consequence increasing to the next wave. And so on. Until the waves end. That is how we are. All our lives beginning and ending with the consequences of being. The consequence of light.

"Sometimes there is a hand, and I know it is mine, or yours, or maybe I just want to be holding on to something willing to share."

Me too. Beyond the page rested centuries of thoughts. And the centuries of thoughts were not this. They were things and air and you can see it when the sun hurts your eyes. Like a blanket wrapping. Like a hand curled into the form of wanting. Like the length of a stick above the sand. Simple as it may seem we are devoted by being. Neither death nor life. Living.

Finding is the act of living. Not finding the lost, but finding.

"Have I known before?"

Before? No. Now. Yes. Before/now. Yes.

Your sense (non)

In hand in. Drop extends to wave.

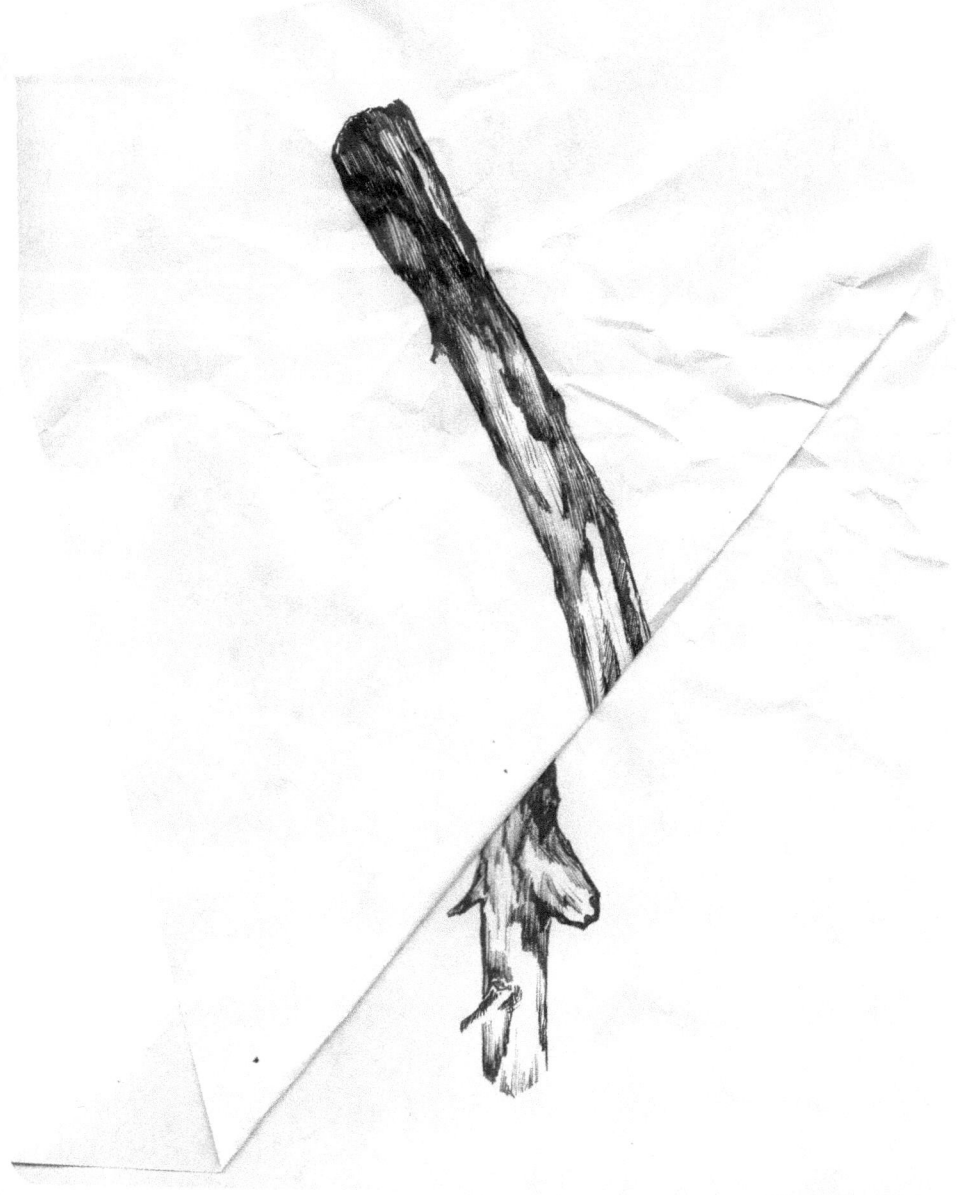

Procuring the same

If longer is tamer than is. Drop is not drop at all.

I knew upon picking it up that it was more beyond than before. It was saturated with the way of the dropping wave. Its caress was moist, like there had been a sinking suspicion of sailing. It floated on waves. Inland than out. Just beyond grasp. Then back. Beckoning a new. and beckoning a position. Changed by its substance I ran it through my hands and could sense each undulation in the wood as if centuries had written their meaning in bark, in lasting softness. In wood. Edges now round. Their perfection found in delicacy and simplicity. I would stare at this for days. My eyes captured by its nothing more than, had an attitude of emulation that suffered me to reposition. The sun, an ally, began its warm intrusion, its graceful blessing one fragment at a time, becoming dry under the conversation of heat. Its preservation needing nothing but. Each piece of shallow ripened and surfaced to expose. The flavor of the interior could be smelt by careful. Each scent apart from the (other than) now happening in all places. A careful showing, whose lesson was expansion through through emptying. Making more than, through hollowness. Feeling through filling.

It was in this moment I could understand what no reaction to act felt like. The now dried stick became and I could see why it fascinated. Its mirror like surface was only an understanding. It preferred the lessons of reaching over the lessons of stale.

Needing to make lasting I developed a plan for presenting. A symbolic nothing. A way to celebrate both living and life. In openness all moments. A monolith for moments. I would perform the ceremony of solitude, and would display it in ordinary.

I took the stick across the sand and found the softest. I placed one end nearly on and then slowly it was taken by the ground. I planted it, but unlike a tree it had no function in up. I know there is no future tree in the planting, but the action became an overture to the day. The planting was a character to becoming something other than. Each character meaning something more than. I knew simply that this felt. I do not know what the name for that is.

Of sorts

Equity maximized outcome. Drop equals all That and Same.

Having launched myself through a day racked with the right and knowing, and, having found, I knew that each morning became a visceral and belonging. My shoes were slightly larger than one half size and sounded fragmented as they collided with the floor in an empty heap. Socks slid on the floor as each step landed where it would have anyway. The pressure of each moment eased into the next, and each wave of understanding dissipated into longer than next. I became something of each and nothing of where. In here I found the exact and the be.

The corner of the mattress sunk slightly more than one half as my weight stretched across its tension. Its support not unlike the idea of buoyancy or floating or stick sliding across each wave in a predictable nonchalance. Predictable until one hand reached across the stretch and rooted the idea in softest sand. The stick became a character. Each character meaning something more than. Each creative endeavor of finding became a momentary swelling, though each moment became the next. And the next became. And the next.

I long to know. I long for feeling and prepared hollowness. As my eyes begin their shifting coda I settled into the comfort of breathing again. The structural conclusion to the story began before the waking. It always had. And yet I found that the cadence was always mine. And precisely yours. And precisely.

Every moment begins in the yester part of longing and finds a way through the pointed peculiarity of expectations. I understand now, what it means to smile in the dark, or to curl my hand in wanting and find sharing.

Slumber settled in and somewhere else a stick, still stuck half a length above, remained a stick. Remained exactly what it had been, and knowing it could, I comforted back into something like a blanket that was nothing like a blanket, but more like a knowing. This was how I spent the rest of the day.

1.

Was it a curse, perhaps, to be named III. Or an attempt to appease the length of pain which really is more like a glance. Perception. Was it so wrong to want to see your eyes?

That's where my story really begins. Somewhere beyond the curse of biting my own tongue. Shaking the limbs of branches and rattling the cages of assumptions I seem to find a reason to be lost in each laugh, and to be lost in each desire to laugh, and to be lost in a breath which so longs to be a desire. Did I tell you that they once gave me a crown? It wasn't a crown really. It was an extra meal. It was a way to make me feel like I had done something well because they wanted me to do it again. That was my introduction to disappointment.

I meant to tell you that I had a wonderful time yesterday. It meant a lot when you came to visit and we talked about the smell of rain. It seems cliche. But, there was that time when I knew the way the wind was going to enter the room because the pain in my hand was too unbearable. You laughed, told me I just need to take a bath. Soak myself with salt. Lick the wound a little and ease back into sense.

When the window broke, and the storm tore the trees I didn't get out of the water.

I learned once how to measure the length of a day. It isn't about the time it takes to walk the circumference. I wouldn't have known that three days ago. It was about the way to encompass the mortar and the fertilizer. It was about the diagram and the entanglement. When they looked at me and said:

"You have to take your pills now."

I didn't really hear the urgency. I needed a way to express necessity.

"You need to explain why you don't want me as your doctor."

That was my introduction to anger.

"You need to take these if you want to leave"

That was my introduction to honesty.

Have you ever held your own hand, just for the company? I think I told you this song was a way to understand sorrow. If you walk the length of the sand the waves lap your toes. Just beyond grasp. What if I told you my day was spent at the threshold of a window. At the edge of believing I could be more than contained, but less than heroic. I pretend that shoe sizes matter, that the air end somehow means I feel the freedom of belonging to more than some colonizing idea.

It turns out that the way to understand sorrow is to carry the myth in the song, or to believe that it is washed in blood.

My father's name was Orpheus. The length of a day suspends like carrion. Is it worth longing for these eyes? A symbolic nothing. A way to celebrate both living and life and not-life and not-living. In openness all moments. A monolith for moments. I would perform the ceremony of solitude, and would display it in ordinary. My father's name was Orpheus.

www.ingramcontent.com/pod-product-compliance
Lightning Source LLC
Chambersburg PA
CBHW070943250626
47159CB00009B/3369